When the Devil

a novelette

EMMA E. MURRAY

SHORTWAVE
PUBLISHING

Content Warnings can be found at the back of this book.

Shortwave Publishing
contact@shortwavepublishing.com
Full Catalog: shortwavepublishing.com

Cover design and interior layout by Alan Lastufka.

First Edition published May 2024.

10 9 8 7 6 5 4 3 2 1

ISBN 978-1-959565-30-7 (paperback)
ISBN 978-1-959565-31-4 (ebook)

When the. Devil

For Mom. I know you'd be proud of me.

one

I MISSED Mawmaw's funeral 'cause I ruined the potatoes. I'd been watching the clouds gather, a soft rain falling as I wiped at my red eyes. I didn't notice the milk had turned. Dumped that clotted mess right in the pot without checking, and there wasn't enough to start again. Travis had watched from across the kitchen, his eyes hot coals, and I remember trying to swallow but my throat was dry, wedged shut.

He went in my place, told 'em all I was too sad to even get out of bed. He relished recounting every detail of their disapproving tongue clicks and raised eyebrows; he lapped up every drop of my pain. I just wanted to say goodbye. At least she didn't see my absence, unless the preacher's right and she's looking down, watching my every move. But Mawmaw would forgive me.

Reality was he couldn't let me be seen for a few

days. Not 'til the twin black eyes resembled the tearstained troughs of an overdramatic granddaughter he'd painted to everyone at the service. At least he never hit me in the face again after that; too hard to hide. He settled for the places hidden under my thin cotton dresses, yellowed under the arms, that wear out as fast as I can make 'em.

The only one who knew the truth was Pawpaw. He didn't let his wife's death stop him from his random check-ins, making sure I wasn't getting into trouble when Travis was out trucking. He took one look at my black-rimmed eyes and fat lip; shook his head. He left right then and there.

At least he left me alone for a while after that. He knew nobody'd be stepping out with a double-barreled bruise like me. Never trusted me that he'd raised an honest woman, even as strict as my grandparents were. What was all the whippin' for if I had to be watched every minute of my life? If I'd learned anything, it's that men never trust a woman any farther than they can throw her, which is hardly across the room, slammed into a wall, still thinking she's about to run off with the first guy who looks her way.

Without Mawmaw, the days crawled by on ragged knees, scorching dry and exhausted. She'd always been the one light in my life, a voice of reason against Pawpaw and even Travis. They often wouldn't listen, but at least she tried. Without her, the visits from Pawpaw were swift and mean. He didn't bring small treats, didn't comb my hair and kiss my cheek, didn't help fold the sheets while we listened to the songbirds. I now struggled with the sheets alone. Most days were lonely, just waiting for the sun to set so I could sleep again. When Travis was home, it wasn't much better. He never had much nice to say.

I was unpinning the laundry, the prickly dead grass poking the soles of my feet, when a truck pulled into the McCallum's driveway. Now, right away I was curious, seeing as Eileen and George McCallum never had any visitors. They kept to themselves, barely acknowledging me when I gave a neighborly hello, so of course I was gonna nose around and find out who would be stopping by.

A young woman got out of the truck, wild dark hair a mess around her shoulders, and I watched as she waved off the driver, holding a bright red suitcase pulled from the bed. Looked about my age, just out of school, but she'd obviously taken the opposite route of me. Tattoos scattered across her arms and wearing combat boots; she was definitely wild. A city girl. I wondered where she came from and couldn't decide if I pitied, hated, or envied her. Maybe a little of each. There was also a spark of something not so dark and yet velvet black, a waft of musky perfume and satin sweet, but I nestled that feeling further back, letting it stay fuzzy and amorphous, out of sight.

The girl marched right in without knocking,

the screen door slapping behind her, and that was that. There wasn't any commotion, so I went back to the laundry and forgot about her. It wasn't until a couple days later, when I'd walked to the Dollar General and saw her again, that I even remembered her existence beyond just another worker in the fields. She was browsing the aisles as I gathered up the couple things I needed, and though I stole a few glimpses of her, I didn't say a word. But as soon as I'd checked out, she caught up, right outside as the heat hit us both like a sticky open palm.

"Chips, cleaning spray, and a toilet brush? That's gotta be the strangest shopping trip I've ever seen." The words were sharp, but her voice poured over me like slow rolling honey. The thick drawl surprised me, and I realized maybe I'd judged her too quick.

"What do you mean?" I asked, face flaming with embarrassment and undeserved shame. "It was only what I needed. Is that so strange?"

"I don't know; guess it's not." She smirked and flitted around me like a gnat. "You live next door, don't ya? What's your name?"

"Um, yeah, if you mean the brown house with the green door, that's mine." Something dropped in my stomach like a stone, sending ripples through my blood. "I'm Libby."

"Nice to meet you, Libby." She grabbed my hand even though it'd just been dangling at my side. "I'm June."

I pulled my hand away by instinct but regretted it immediately. It felt surprisingly nice to be touched, not in the harsh, selfish way Travis did, but in a firm, yet gentle, way. One corner of my mouth pulled up in the faintest smile as I remembered how Mawmaw would grab my hands, pulling me along when she was excited to show me something, a newly finished embroidery or the first blossom that opened in her garden. June's eager hands opened a door of memories that flooded forward; I struggled to close it and return to the moment.

We walked for a while down the sidewalk, not talking but headed the same direction home. The air was humid, dewing up my skin and frizzing my hair. After almost tripping on a cracked bit of concrete, tufts of grass between the slabs catching my foot, I hissed a curse and June giggled. I wasn't mad. Her laugh was nice, even with the little snort at the end.

"So, you're helping around the farm there, right?" I asked.

"Sure. I needed some money and so they're letting me work part time. Stay for free in the extra room, though it's just a cot on the floor."

The way June shrugged, the sunlight seemed to slip off her bare shoulders, soaking into the faded tank top and adding a subtle glow to her skin. I realized I was staring and quickly looked ahead, careful not to trip again.

"You live by yourself in that house?" she asked.

"Nah, but sometimes it feels like it." I laughed. "Travis is always out truckin' so he's not home very much."

"You work?"

"Oh, no, Travis would never want me to. He works hard and makes good money. He likes me to stay home and keep it tidy. I grow some of our food in the garden, and sometimes I sell pies and cookies, but mostly I'm just a housewife. That's what makes him happy."

I tried to smile but found the corners of my mouth wouldn't cooperate. June furrowed her brows.

"Kids?"

"No, not yet. Thank God." I straightened at the slip, charged with a cold like an icicle down my spine. Stumbling over my tongue, I added, "But I'm sure we'll be blessed soon enough. Travis always wanted a big family."

June just raised her eyebrow and nodded, the ghost of a smirk still on her lips.

"Say, what're you up to today? Besides laundry and bullshit like that," she asked.

"Guess nothing much."

"Well, today's my day off and I got a joint and bottle of Jim, if you wanna hang out." Her eyes shimmered like an asphalt mirage.

"Okay," I said before I had time to second-guess myself.

two

ON THE BACK PATIO, sitting in the rust-stained chairs, I watched the clouds roll by and smiled. It was the most relaxed I'd felt in a couple years, maybe longer. I couldn't remember the last time I'd felt that happy, even without the other stuff.

"Tell me why you decided to tie yourself down in this shithole town, young and pretty like you are?" June asked, leaning forward, elbows on the outstretched dusty knees of her jeans and the neck of the bottle in her hand.

"That's a bit harsh, don't ya think?" I shot back, but the way she grinned with her eyes calmed me down. "I mean, sure, it's not really what I thought my life would be. Mawmaw caught us messin' around when I was still in school, and Pawpaw marched me down the aisle with a gun at my back." I sniffed out a laugh, but June didn't join me. "Not really, of course! It's just a joke. But he certainly wasn't gonna have people finding out, especially if I wound up knocked up or something, and so I suppose I didn't really have much of a choice. Travis isn't all bad though. He takes care of me as best as he can, works his ass off to make sure we have nice things, and I 'ppreciate that."

"That's sad as fuck. You didn't get to live any kind of life at all before getting shackled to that man."

My eyes slit as I grabbed the bottle from her hand and took a long swig, savoring the burn down my throat.

"It's really not so bad as you think," I said, but the way the words stuck on my tongue, I didn't even convince myself.

"Don't get all teary on me now. It's not like there's no hope." That mischievous aura returned around her; the sun haloed behind her wild mane. "I bet I could find a way or two to bring some excitement into your life."

The butterflies tumbling in my stomach were edged with the metallic tang of guilt. I hadn't done anything too wrong, just drinking with a new friend, but bubbling below the surface, the sin called to me.

I brushed the guilt away. I hadn't done nothing, and I would keep it that way. I had to stay strong like they taught in the teen Bible group. But I reassured myself there wasn't too much wrong in daydreams, not as long as I kept 'em clean as I could.

"So, why are you stayin' with the McCallums? They don't seem like your kind of people, you know?"

June's mouth flinched as I changed the subject, but she didn't hide from the question. "Well, whether I like it or not, they *are* my people. Eileen's my aunt. Mom's sister. I didn't necessarily want to come out here, but Dad kicked me out the first chance he got, and after they found Mom on the railroad tracks, torn to pieces, that was his chance. I saw it with my own eyes when the thing hit her."

My eyes bugged, mouth hung open, but I snapped a hand over it as shame washed over me for prying.

"That's terrible. I'm so sorry."

"Eh, she was drunk as a skunk and had it coming. Didn't break my heart a bit, to be honest."

The ice in her voice ran my blood cold as a lizard.

"Come on now. That's your own momma you're talking about. You should have a little respect for the dead."

"She didn't earn my respect." Her eyes caught mine and each word stung like a wasp bite. "You didn't know her, so don't pretend to understand."

"Sorry." The apology was hushed, barely audible, but June accepted it right away, any trace of ire falling away with a blink.

"Anyway, none of that matters anymore. I'm on my own now. Dad said I was grown and needed to start my life already, but I knew my aunt needed some help on the farm, so I figured I might as well stop here for a bit and save up some cash to make it easier when I head on out."

"That's nice of your aunt, though I saw you out there yesterday. They work you hard." I paused, hesitating but the liquor brought the words out anyway. "I never thought the McCallums seemed like nice people to be honest. Never wave back or smile. But I guess I was wrong, with them taking you in like that, giving you some honest work."

June barked out a loud laugh, startling me, but I couldn't help but join her.

"No, you weren't wrong, Lib. They're assholes," she said, and we both broke down, braying with laughter and gasping for air.

As I laughed, a light rain dotted my pink dress with mauve and worked at taming down my stray hairs. June wiped at her cheeks just as a big drop landed on the tip of her nose. The sky stayed robin's egg blue; the sun not even obscured by the few clouds in the sky.

"I love it when it's like this," I said, holding my palms up to catch the cool drops.

"Like what?"

"When the Devil beats his wife."

"What the fuck's that 'sposed to mean?" she asked, face scrunching into a tight sneer.

"You've never heard that before? My momma didn't get time to teach me much, but that's one thing she did. That's the name for rain when the sun's out. Never thought much about it."

"Your momma was wrong. That's a sun shower."

The way she said it took me aback and I just mumbled, "Whatever."

I stared up at the sky, the wisps of clouds crying on me with the cerulean sky behind it, bright and dancing with sunlight. The buzz was getting to me, my head dizzy, floating like a balloon, giddy and wild. I reached out my hands again, catching more drops, but my elbow accidentally nudged the bottle off the armrest where I'd set it, glass clattering across the concrete. My breath caught in my throat as I jumped to my feet, snatching up the shattered remains. Jagged edges gleamed at me where the neck split, drops of rain landing on my face, threatening the misting of my eyes to gather and fall.

"I'm sorry!" I whimpered, bracing for the assault, either verbal or physical. I spun around, but June's eyes sparkled along with the sweet melody of her laugh.

"More like when the Devil gets drunk before dinner, huh?" She stretched her arms back, clasping them behind her head. "Now I wouldn't say no to another round for you and me both, whatcha think? I saw you had a six-pack in the fridge. Hell, grab one for the Devil while you're at it."

A timid smile crawled over my lips, but I dashed it away. Hiding the bottle behind my back, I straightened up, her words tumbling through me.

"You shouldn't joke about the Devil, you know. He's always watching; listening. Didn't they teach you that in church?"

"Lib, there's no fucking Devil." She spit the words out and they splattered on the dirt between us. "And there ain't no God neither."

"How can you say that?" My skin prickled in a blush as I whispered, as if God couldn't hear us if we spoke low and soft enough.

"You've gotta be your own God in this fucked up world. That's the only way to be happy." There wasn't a tremble of doubt in her voice, and it pulled the breath from my lungs, leaving me speechless.

three

I PLUCKED at the lilac dress that nearly drowned me in frills and fabric, finally belting it with a stretch of ribbon to give me a little more shape. I didn't need to rouge my cheeks, already sunburn red with some mixture of shame and excitement. When I looked in the mirror, the feelings intensified. I carefully applied the plum lipstick I'd swiped from Mawmaw long ago and brushed out my hair.

June was in the McCallum's front yard, her hair wet and slicked back out of her face, not dressed up at all in stained denim overalls, but I didn't mind. I still thought she looked nice, and when I got close, I liked how she smelled of citrus shampoo and cut grass.

"Why're you all dolled up?"

"I don't know. Sometimes I just like to, and I don't usually got a reason. Thought it might be fun, I guess." I shrugged like I didn't care. June just snorted a laugh.

I didn't walk to the theater, I floated, and throughout the movie, I couldn't keep my eyes on the screen. Not daring to look at June, my gaze moved between the film and her hands which rested together in her lap. Over and over, I imagined slipping my own between them, but I didn't. I couldn't even move until the credits started rolling and the lights came on.

We talked about dumb nothings the whole way until we got to her aunt's house.

"Thanks again for coming to the movies with me. Beats going alone."

"Of course," I said, too fast and flustered, my face crimson even in the dark.

"I'd love to see you again sometime." Her voice was a rumble of faraway thunder.

"Anytime!" I could've slapped myself for the eager trill of an answer. "Travis probably won't be home for a few more days, maybe even a week, so I've got nothin' but time."

June nodded and we stood at the end of the driveway for a long moment. Then she leaned forward and kissed me. Just a quick peck on the lips, so fast I couldn't even think to kiss back, and then she was halfway to her aunt's house. My eyes followed her inside, but she didn't turn around once. That night I prayed for my soul, but my dreams were filled with the sweet scent of June.

The earliest hours of a new day were alive with cicadas and moths battering the bedroom window where I never blew out the candle. I couldn't get back to sleep. For the tenth time that night, I walked across the room to look out at the McCallum's place. June was in the window, framed perfect as a picture. Her eyes burned through me. I wasn't myself when I pulled my nightgown over my head, my view a gossamer blue for a moment. June was still there, watching me. She didn't smile, didn't move. I felt like a different person altogether standing nearly nude in the window, the first rays of sunrise dancing down skin that'd never seen anything but dark.

My fingers tiptoed up June's stomach, but she brushed my hand away.

"That tickles!"

"Sorry, I'll stop." I grinned and she play punched my bare arm.

"So, you're serious? He's really been your only one?"

"Yeah. I mean, I kissed a bit with a couple other boyfriends, but nothing more than that. Well, then Travis comes along, we got caught, and that was it. Everybody was so afraid of a baby, but one never came. Though wouldn't be surprised if Trav has a few little ones out there. Lord knows he's brought back a couple things that had me blushing at the doctor's so he's definitely not wrapping it up while he's out sowing his seeds."

June stared hard at me. I flinched a little under her gaze.

"What a goddamn bastard. How can he treat you like that?"

"That's just how it is with most men, June. Don't play dumb."

"It don't have to be like that, Lib."

"Of 'course it does. This ain't no fairytale world. You know that better than anyone."

"Yeah, but there's ways to get what you want. You're just scared to step outta the circle your grandaddy drew for you."

"Take that back."

"Sure, I'll take it back, when you show me I'm wrong."

My heart swelled up like I was bursting with something to say back, but when I opened my mouth, there was nothing. Instead, June pushed her face close, and I welcomed her tongue as it slid against my own.

<hr>

The night wind brushed across my face as I sat on the porch swing, looking out at the dirt and small pebbles from the road whip up, tumbling for a moment before settling again. The dancing stones reminded me of June. So did the yellow glow of the moon. So did the touch of the breeze like fingers through my hair. So did the canopy of stars glittering across the depths of space. I sighed, sinking into myself, and wishing I could think about anything else, but everything was June.

Darker thoughts burned like embers at the base of my skull. What we were doing was a sin. A terrible sin that would be punished with hellfire and eternal damnation. I was cheating on Travis, a full-blown adulterer, and with a woman at that. My jaw ached and I realized I'd been grinding my teeth. I forced my muscles to relax, but the pain remained, and now my attention was brought to my mouth. The lips, tongue, gently nipping teeth that teased my sweet June. No, I snapped myself out of the daydream. It was wrong. I was a bad person. A sinner.

But then Travis seeped to the forefront of my mind with a shudder. He was always stepping out on me, and yet he seemed as sure as a preacher that he was going to be welcomed right in through those pearly gates. I bit at my lip, rolling my eyes at his dumb excuses when I'd ask where he'd been, what had happened to the money, and why he came home with a waft of choking floral perfume. Sometimes he wouldn't even bother to lie, just ignore me, maybe slap me around a bit. Tell me it's none of my business what a man does and not a wife's place to even dare ask.

I scoffed at the sky, clear and cloudless. If God was up there, I wanted him to answer for all the bullshit that was men and their arrogant self-importance. Were they really blessed to be so much more powerful, stronger, and untouchable than women? Why did He play favorites, leaving us to grovel at undeserving feet before they kick out our teeth and laugh? I clasped my hands together, cinched my eyes tight, and prayed as hard as I'd ever prayed. Tell me God, is love like this a sin? Is Travis forgiven and I'm cursed? Give me some kind of sign to tell me June's wrong and You're up there, looking out for me, preparing my place in heaven, and I'll stop sinning with her, no matter how much it hurts.

I waited and waited, watching the stars twinkle and the wind shake the trees, but there was no sign. No booming angel's voice, not a single cricket. No bright flash across the sky, not even a faint shooting star. I watched with bated breath for as long as I could, until all my patience and hope had run out like the sand in an hourglass, collecting around my feet with wilted apathy. Then I went inside, curled up under the quilt, and fell into a deep, dreamless sleep. He didn't even come to me in my dreams. Not even then.

four

THE MIDDAY HEAT was tolerable under the canopy of trees in the bit of greenbelt behind the high school, my old hangout. Shadows dappled the grass we lay on as we passed the blunt back and forth.

"My back is killing me. They work me like a fucking mule," June said, groaning and turning to her side to face me.

"Yeah, I saw you out there seedin' while I was pullin' weeds in the garden. Maybe you should get a job in town instead. Wouldn't you rather work as a cashier with the AC blastin' than out on the fields?"

June took a deep inhale of smoke, held it, and then let it out long and slow.

"Hell no."

The giggle in my throat was cut off by the rustling of someone coming through the bushes.

"Fuck, nobody comes out here," I hissed, scrambling to my feet. I was already slipping between trees when I heard June behind me.

"What are you doing?"

I looked back at her. She stood in the same spot, her face twisted in puzzlement.

"Come on, we've gotta hide."

"I'm not gonna hide," June said, slowly rising after stamping out the cherry. "There's nobody out here, Lib. Calm down."

But I didn't wait for her, already moving through some roots to a vantage point obscured by leaves. Just then, an asshole everyone called Buck pushed through some branches. He'd been a hotshot in school, but as soon as we all moved on, he soured into a nasty, washed-up nobody. Now he spent all his time trying to pick up high schoolers at the gas station he worked at by offering to overlook their age and sell them beer. A real piece of shit. Most everyone steered clear.

I knew June would pick up on it right away, despite having never met him in her life. He even smelled a little off, like something rotting from the inside. I only noticed it after school ended, and I remembered wondering if that smell was his desperation to be admired again seeping through, gone moldy and bitter like we'd all gone on him. She'd smell it on him, but even as strong and independent as June was, my heart leaped behind my tongue, drumming against the back of my throat as my mind whispered *run, run, run.*

"Damn girl, you've been smokin' it up back here, huh?" he said as he strode into the clearing like he had every right to be there.

"What's it to you?"

"Jeez, you don't gotta be like that. I just smelled something nice out here and decided to take a look." He eyed her up and down. "You're the new farmhand at the McCallum's right? I think I seen you around."

"Yeah, that's me." June stood rigid yet there was that languid ease to her movements, like a snake's warning dance before it strikes. Still, there was a hint of fear in the dark of her eyes, and I thought of when my momma once told me snakes don't snap to be mean, but just 'cause they're protecting themselves.

"Have anything left to share with a new friend?" He moved a little closer, forcing June to take a step back.

"Nah, and I wouldn't even if I did. Now, I just wanna be alone if you don't mind."

"Well, I hear you, but I've been hoping for a little company. Pretty girl like you seems like someone nice to spend the afternoon with." I watched his tongue dart out and lick his lips. June noticed too, a sneer rising on one side of her mouth, but she just shook her head and turned away, walking back toward the brush that separated the small circle of trees from the trail.

Buck followed after, nearly stepping on her heels he was so close, but she didn't speed up.

"Come on. Why're you doing this? We both know I'm not your type and you're definitely not mine."

"How would you know my type?" He grinned, leaning closer.

"I just do, and I'm not it." She grinned back, but there was not a drop of playfulness in hers.

"Maybe you're not my usual kind of girl, but you look fun." I flinched as his greasy fingers reached up, running through June's dark tangle of hair, but she didn't move, stood as still and strong as a statue. "I bet you've had a lot of fun in your life."

"Oh yeah, tons, but I won't be having none with you."

"Maybe you'd change your mind for a price." Pinched between his fingers were folded green, and though I couldn't tell how much from how far I was, I was sure it wouldn't be near enough to make her even pause. And yet, her eyes flashed to the cash and back to meet his eyes. My lips mouthed "no," but there was nothing I could do.

"I know your kind, and there's always a price." He stepped closer again, pressing her nearer to the tree line. "Or maybe you'd rather play a little game, make me catch you. It's up to you. Whatcha say?"

"Hmm, so those are my choices, huh? You should've led with that," she gestured to the hand holding the money, "if you were offering," June purred, but there was something harsh and bright in her eyes. "Mind if we have a drink first? In my experience, it loosens everyone's nerves to their benefit."

"Hell yeah, sweetheart. I've never turned down a drink before," he laughed, and as soon as June's hand emerged from her bag with the Gatorade bottle, he'd snatched it from her grasp, already unscrewing it. "Some kind of vodka mix?" He took a swig, face screwing up tight, before she answered, examining the label. "I like the disguise, heh."

"Yeah, my aunt don't like me drinkin' so I hide it best I can," she answered, her eyes narrow as Buck took another long gulp. After wiping his mouth, he handed the bottle back to her, but June didn't drink. She just screwed the orange top back on, her eyes never leaving his face.

"You ain't having none?" He wiped at his mouth again, but his eyes now locked with June's steady stare. "You know, that tasted kinda funny. What all you put in there?"

June absolutely beamed as she shrugged her shoulders, and then in an instant, Buck was hunched over himself, retching in the bushes.

"Augh, my stomach's killin' me. What the fuck'd you give me?" He batted at her with a limp arm, but she easily stepped out of his reach before he crumpled to the ground, strings of vomit trailing to the grass. "What was it?" he demanded again between choking coughs, but she just shrugged, that eerie grin still plastered from cheek to cheek.

Then she was giggling, even as he begged her for water, crawling toward her, his fingers digging past plants, clawing into the black dirt. Buck spasmed twice as he flipped onto his back then stiffened, every muscle twitching and his eyes rolling in his head, a thick white foam filling his mouth until it spilled over, dribbling down his cheek, puddling under his head.

It only lasted a few minutes, June and me both watching as he gurgled in pain before he stopped moving, every part of him becoming fully relaxed. A wet patch appeared at the crotch of his jeans and the air filled with a faint smell of overripe fruit and urine. June stopped her laughter with a hand over her mouth, walking close enough to nudge him with the toe of her boot. Buck didn't move. His chest didn't rise.

"When the Devil drinks your Gatorade. Am I right, Lib?" June laughed, eyes sparkling in the dappled light filtered through leaves, as if she'd only been playing an innocent prank. I couldn't comprehend.

I stepped into the middle of the clearing, where the trees opened and let the noon sun beat down on my face while I squinted at the body. Despite the heat, a shiver flew over my skin, and I shook my head, shooing it away. June bent over, taking the wad of cash from his already paling hand, counting through it quickly before shoving it in her pocket.

"You killed him?" I asked it like a question, but I had no doubt, and even saying the words, I couldn't grasp beyond the unreality of it all.

"Aw, don't look like that." June set a heavy hand on my shoulder. "Come on. What's it really matter? You ever thought about how we all live and die so quick, time barely blinks an eye before we're gone."

"But—"

"Don't you try to tell me he wouldn't've taken me out just as easy without a lick of remorse if he'd seen an opportunity. And the law'd be on his side. They'd just think I'm some whore, even though I've never done nothing like that in my life. A woman can't dress how she wants or think for herself without being labeled a whore, and once you're a whore, you're trash. Well, I won't have it. That's why I'm always prepared. Little rat poison and pesticide does the trick." She shook the bottle. "Lib, the world's my oyster and I'm gonna be a god who takes what I want until I'm snuffed out and disappear into the ether of it all."

She'd worked herself up to the point she was panting, eyes gone wild like an angry dog, but I wasn't afraid. I pawed at her with a passion I'd never felt in my whole life, and from below, Buck looked up at our sin with blind eyes full of sky.

five

I SWORE to myself I wouldn't see her anymore. She was more than a sinner; she was a murderer. That word bounced in my stomach, a nauseous clump, every time the memory of those lifeless eyes full of sky wormed its way into my mind. And yet, when I thought of June, it wasn't Buck's corpse that came to me but her smirking rosebud pout and tender hands, surprisingly soft despite the hard work she put them through, her dirty fingernails bitten down to the quick. I could nearly smell her intoxicating mix of fresh air, cut grass, and warm cinnamon musk just by pretending she was there with me, breathing deeply into the pillow where she'd rested her head next to mine. Something more than lust quivered and pulsed through my veins, nipping at me like crawling fire ants and keeping me up all night, torn between what I'd seen and what I wanted.

The longer I contemplated it, the more I convinced myself that June had been left with no other options. The world would have had her run away, maybe scratch and kick, but ultimately cower and give in, even die at his hand rather than fight back. And hadn't that been what she'd done in a way? Preemptively taking back the power he'd sought to assert? I knew I was stretching my morality cobweb thin, but I couldn't help but have a little admiration. I'd never seen a woman be so clever and cruel. Thinking of her eyes shining as she looked at me, elven in her coyness, melted my heart all over again. I couldn't stay away. The power that oozed from her every pore was irresistible. And then there I was at her window, gently tapping in the earliest hours of the day, like a moth drawn to her light. She let me in without a word or even a smile. We made love then I crawled back out into the golden morning, slightly ashamed but fully satisfied.

Three days of sheer bliss followed. I forced myself to flush Buck from my memory. It helped that the cops didn't even go looking for him 'til he'd been missing two days and his momma got worried, and then I heard through the smalltown grapevine that they didn't find his death at all suspicious when they found him. Turns out paraquat and cyanide suicides aren't all that rare out in the country, even if it's a rough way to go. Cheap and easy, a lot more people swallow deadly cocktails than you'd ever guess. I couldn't believe they just accepted it and moved on, and it was even crazier how easy it was to keep on living as if nothing had happened at all. The memory faded rapidly over those first few days, June's smile so bright it overexposed all the worst parts of each day into white emptiness, leaving me with only thoughts of her spitting beer across the table as she laughed, watching her through the window as she worked in the field, and the dark velvet of her tongue slipping between my lips.

We talked about everything but never Buck, never what had happened in the woods. I liked pretending it had nothing to do with us. It was easier that way. Everything was easier with June.

"Tell me your life story," she said, my dress pulled up and cheek against the rise and fall of my soft stomach. I'd laughed, but when her brow knitted together, I knew she was serious. I regurgitated the basics, but she begged for more. Next came a tearful tread down the worn memories with Mawmaw, the couple fuzzy toddlerhood recollections of my mother before she ran off, and the minor achievements I'd collected over my short life: student of the month in middle school, second place in the fifth-grade talent show for my dance routine, the blue ribbon I won at state for the goat Pawpaw gifted me and helped me raise.

When those didn't satisfy her, I frowned and sat up.

"I don't have much of a story to tell. What do you think I'm holding back?" I couldn't hide the annoyance in my voice and when June sat up, I shrank from her, expecting a slap to put me back in line, but instead she pulled me to her, held me against her chest.

"Tell me something you've never told anyone. Something hidden deep down, something secret." Her eyes twinkled as she traced a finger down my inner thigh.

"I don't really have any secrets like that to—"

As I was speaking, the front door squealed open and then slammed shut. We both sat up straight, and I ran my hands down the wrinkled front of my dress, pulling it down and quietly thanking God that we were both fully clothed.

"Libby! Where you at, girl?" Pawpaw called from the living room, his voice rough like his calloused hands.

"Coming!" I shouted back, scurrying to the door, but he was already standing in the doorframe by the time I'd stood up.

"What're y'all doing back here?" His eyes roved our bodies, searching for signs of the sin that settled unspoken in the stale air between us.

"Nothing, sir. We were just talking," June piped up behind me, and I looked back at her, surprised at her smug grin even though I suspected it from her tone.

Pawpaw narrowed his eyes, staring down June, but she just smiled back, unintimidated.

"And who are you?"

June didn't offer her hand, didn't stand up, didn't move at all. She just smiled, her eyes sharp as knives, leaning back, propped by her elbows.

"I'm the new farmhand next door. Name's June."

"Hmm," Pawpaw grunted, still eyeing her. "I'd heard they were lookin' for someone. Interestin' the McCallums would hire. . . someone like you."

June's smirk never faltered.

"Yeah, but I'm strong as a bull. Just as good at the work as any man." Her eyes flickered to me with a feline stealth, sending an electric pulse down my spine. "Plus, Eileen's my aunt."

I noticed Pawpaw's shoulders relax just slightly, the leather of his face softening.

"Ah, I see."

That was all he needed to hear. I could tell he thought he understood everything about June and a fury burned in my belly at his assumptions, but I didn't let a spark of it show. He turned his attention back to me, and I immediately shrank under his gaze.

"Lib, I don't like finding you lounging around like. . ." He looked to June then back to me. "This.

It ain't proper, and just 'cause you're grown don't mean I can't send you out to cut a switch, got it?"

"Yes, sir."

"Now your friend best be getting back to work and you start—"

June's voice cut through his words, catching him off guard.

"Work's done for the day."

His jaw hung slack for a moment then he snapped it shut and I swear I could see the red flaming behind his irises.

"Don't you talk back to your elders, young lady. You need to be getting back to yours. Libby's got housework to do." His eyes were filled with constrained disgust and rage when he looked back to me. "You ne'er know when Travis will get home. You should be preparing a good dinner just in case."

When he noticed June hadn't budged, his back went rigid again and through clenched teeth he added, "Actually, I think I'll join you for dinner, Lib. So you best be starting. It's already getting dark." He looked between us again. "Unless you're looking for a whoopin'. Is that what you want?" He coughed a dry, crackling laugh. "Answer me, girl."

"No, sir." My voice was robotic and distant, a cold shame unrolling across my skin as June stood up and left. I kept my eyes down, but the weight of her footsteps told me everything I needed to know.

six

IT ONLY TOOK a day or two for us to develop our own little routine. She'd come over after work in the afternoon and we'd fool around, get drunk and happy, until she stumbled back to her aunt's place. She never stayed over. That was the only thing that could've made it better, but I was always wary that Travis could show back up. I never knew his schedule exactly. I think he liked to keep me on my toes. I just knew he'd be back soon and stay a couple days to recover after such a long haul. I dreaded it with every ounce of my soul.

That night she'd stayed later than usual, and we were a mess of intertwined limbs when headlights shone through the sheer curtains, lighting up the bedroom, sweeping shadows across the floor. I nearly fell out of bed, pulling on my clothes and patting down my hair. June didn't hurry but sighed, moving slow as she smoothed out the sheets.

Gravel rumbled under the weight of the tires as the bobtailed truck pulled close to the house. I ran out to greet Travis, fidgeting with my dress.

Stepping down from the cab, he lit up right away, sucking too hard so the paper sizzled as it burned.

"Hi hon," I said, a smile flickering on my lips. "Good to have you home."

"Did ya miss me?" he asked, pecking my cheek and letting me catch a whiff of whisky breath, but I didn't let my nose wrinkle up and let on I noticed.

"Of course, sweetheart. I always miss you when you're on the road."

"So, this is the famous Travis I've heard so much about." June was behind me in the door frame, her voice startling me. She sauntered out between us, and I wondered if her swagger was for his benefit or my own. Something akin to jealousy bubbled in the pit of my stomach, but I knew I had no right to feel that way.

I hated the way his eyes followed the sway of her hips, his face aglow with the light from inside the house and tip of the cigarette.

"You a friend of Libby's?" He didn't hide the way his eyes slid down her figure.

"Yeah, close friend." She extended a hand. "June." She tossed her hair toward her aunt's house and added, "I'm a farmhand over at the Mc-Callum's."

"You? Working over there?" He slapped his thigh as his face crinkled red with laughter. "You're kidding."

"I ain't no kidder, but you don't have to believe me. Doesn't matter either way."

I saw all the playfulness run right out of his face. He looked waxy pale with the half-moon shining down on us, and even his cigarette seemed to fade to monochrome as frustration seethed from his pores. He wasn't used to a woman talking back, and I could tell by the lines on his forehead that he wasn't sure if he saw her as a challenge or a threat.

"What're y'all doing so late?" He turned to me, lip snarled. "You drinking again? You know I won't have a lush for a wife."

"Nah, I was just bored outta my mind is all, and Libby was keeping me company." June was between us again, moving closer to Travis but she stopped to throw me a wink over her shoulder. "Lib, how 'bout you go inside and finish making that tea."

"Okay." I moved to the living room, where I could watch out the window. Wiping my palms down my dress, I dripped with cold sweat, unsure of what would happen next.

A fake laugh burst into the night as June fawned over my husband. Stealthily, she moved a friendly hand on his shoulder to a more intimate position against his chest. She leaned closer, asking something I couldn't hear, and then I held my breath as they climbed into the truck.

I slipped outside, watching them through the windshield. She was laughing, stroking his hair, saying things I couldn't hear, and then I saw her pull her purse into her lap. The same bottle I'd seen in that sunny clearing in the woods was tenderly held in her fingers, the blue-green liquid sloshing against the plastic sides.

He took it without hesitation, and as I watched him unscrew the orange cap, I knew I should cry out, run to him, stop him somehow. It was the moral thing to do. But I didn't do a thing.

He took a long swig, wiping the glistening green excess on his lips against his sleeve before handing it back. I saw them talking and he didn't seem to notice when she replaced the lid without drinking herself. His hands slid across her stomach and up her chest. He grabbed her breast, clenched it with that familiar clawing lust that made me wince, pushed his face toward hers, but she turned away, only giving him access to her neck. Then I saw his face change.

Coughing violently, he grabbed at June, but she slipped out of his grasp, throwing her head back with a real laugh that glittered like broken glass. Vomit spurted across the dash and soaked through his shirt. My fingers slipped into my mouth, and I bit my cuticles raw as I watched him suffer.

Travis fell forward, convulsing just the same as Buck. After a final rigid shudder, he went still. I hadn't moved, couldn't look away, but when my paralysis broke, I looked to June. Her gaze met mine through the windshield and she smiled. Not a cruel smile, but a tender one, almost bashful, like when you catch your school crush's eye across the classroom. I felt myself hover just above the scene, creating a distance between my mind and body, as if I were only watching a TV drama unfold, not something real, raw, and bleeding.

June stepped down from the truck. A fine spatter of green dotted her face from Travis' dying cough, but she glowed golden beneath in the warm light pouring out from the door. She shrugged a little, still smiling sheepishly.

"Did you. . . ?" My voice was muffled and distant, like it belonged to someone else.

"When the Devil can't keep his dirty paws off you, right?" She laughed a dry forced bark. "I did what needed to be done. That's all."

"No."

She stepped closer. I wanted to run away, crawl under the bedframe and hide, but I couldn't move.

"Libby, don't look so scared. It's going to be okay." My stomach twisted at the way she cooed.

"He didn't do—"

"Stop it," she snapped. "He did plenty."

"But how could you—"

"Easy," was all she answered. My head spun and I clung to the doorframe as I breathed through the nausea.

"We're gonna burn for this," I murmured, but she shook her head and smiled.

"Don't you worry 'bout him or the truck. I'll take them somewhere and deal with what needs to be taken care of. They'll never catch us."

"You can drive a truck like that?" I asked, my voice still a sound from far away, outside my body. I couldn't hide the impressed surprise that trembled through the fear.

June wrinkled up her nose like a bunny and bit her tongue at me, like we were just having fun together again.

"Yeah, sure can. I'm full of surprises."

It was still dark when I heard a car door slam followed by footsteps down the gravel driveway next door. In the gray between late night and early morning, I could make out June's silhouette.

I'd wrestled with myself all night, knowing I should call the cops and turn her in but every time I looked at my phone, my mind settled into an indifferent acceptance. I hadn't loved Travis. Maybe I thought I did at one point early on, but infatuation fades fast and there'd been little affection left after two years of dishonesty and disrespect. June had been wrong, coldblooded, evil even, and yet, there was not one drop of remorse in my heart. Only a soup skin of learned obligation and a twinge of sorrow for his mother, though he only called her once or twice a year. The hardest part would be explaining to Pawpaw that he wasn't coming back, but my thoughts were already weaving themselves into believable lies to spoon-feed whoever asked. I knelt by the edge of my bed and prayed as hard as I could, but God stayed quiet as always. Not even a subtle sign that He disapproved. All I wanted was a sign of something, but it never came. By the time the roosters started shrieking at the pink streaked sky, I'd let go of all apprehensions and embraced the gift June'd given me, sleeping easy and deep while I dreamed of what'd come next.

"Travis. . . he's not coming home. He left me."

"What." Pawpaw's tone was distant and cold, not a question but a flat word to dam the disgust and rage building between his clenched teeth.

"He texted me last night. Said he's found another woman. That bastard."

"Language," Pawpaw growled.

"But he is. Always has been." The venom in my throat was even beginning to convince myself. "Anyhow, he said he ain't coming back. Not even to pick up his things, not that he ever kept much here." Then, with the slightest hesitation, I added, "And he said I could keep the money in the joint account 'til I used it all up. He called it a peace offering."

Pawpaw just watched, the muscles in his jaw working so hard, I wouldn't've been surprised if they'd burst like rubber bands. The longer we stood, the harder it was to keep back the tears, and finally they broke free, wave of soggy sob after sob.

"What am I gonna do now?"

He stood stoic as before, watching me from below drooped eyelids, a web of wrinkles cinched together around his slit eyes.

"Don't surprise me one bit. I don't even know why you're crying. You never did right by him." He walked slow but his feet were heavy on the floor, making sure I heard him leaving over my hollering. "You better start looking for a job 'cause that generous gift he left you will run out sooner than you probably think."

I called after him, but the words were a jumble of snot and snorts. He was already in his truck, backing down the driveway, before I could get to the door to watch him leave.

At the kitchen table, I rested my eyes against my palms and shook. The sound of crying came from my throat, my lungs, my diaphragm, but there weren't any tears. I wasn't sad, only scared. Afraid of what would come next. Afraid of being on my own. Afraid of every little mote of worry that dashed back and forth in my brain, but I couldn't be sad. Not when I was finally free to choose whatever kind of life I wanted. But as I sat with my head in my hands, I felt like a child all over again: endless possibilities ahead of me but all I wanted was to bury my head in my momma's lap and be hushed to sleep.

"So, what'd you do with him?"

June just beamed at me from over the fence.

"Don't you worry 'bout it."

The handle of the trowel nearly slipped free from my sweaty palm.

"I'll see you later. I've gotta get back to work." She started toward the field, but I shouted after her. She stopped, taking a long time to turn back to me. The smile had run away, leaving her face grave and empty.

"What?" she asked.

"I'm scared."

"I told you not to worry about it."

A bird sang in the branches hanging over the fence between us. Sweat beaded on my upper lip and ran from below June's hat, down her temple and cheek.

"Now that I have money, should we leave town?" I asked.

"That'd be too suspicious. And there ain't no need."

"But then we could be together."

"We're together now just fine. Plus, I'll only be here for a little while longer anyhow. I've saved up my own money and I'm getting antsy."

"Would you take me with you?"

"Maybe. Just enjoy the life you're living right now and don't worry 'bout the future."

"But we could have a real future somewhere."

"Libby, you're sweet but you don't know much about anything, do you? Life's just two sides of a coin: violence and pleasure. There's no other point to it. You'll learn to just take what you want and savor the moment, or you'll end up like all the women you've ever known your whole life." I started to answer but she stopped me. "No. Don't say anything. Swallow that down and think on it. I'll come over tonight if you want."

I nodded, turning away before the tears on my eyelashes could overflow down my cheeks.

seven

THE WEATHERMAN SAID a big storm was on the way so I made sure to secure everything I couldn't bring in and lined up the potted plants inside along the sliding door. The last rain had trickled through the roof Travis never got around to replacing, so I set the stockpot where the floor had warped and set to work frying chicken for when June finally finished up and came over.

"Smells good in here," June said, bringing the fragrance of earth and heavy air in with her.

"You said it was your favorite. I made an extra spicy rub."

She smiled, pulled up a chair and watched as I took out the last wings. The wind picked up, whipping at the windows, and the patter of rain across the hungry fields tapped like a soft melody. I sighed when I heard the first drops make their way through the ceiling, dropping into the pot I was thankful I'd put out.

"Made a mash and salad too," I said, sliding the two bowls across the wood.

"You're too good to me." She looked up at me, her face framed by a mop of dark tresses, and I would've forgiven her for anything.

Sitting down, I started dishing out some potatoes, when I heard the slam of the front door through the living room. I started, standing up and the spoon clattering to the floor.

"Libby, get over here."

I knew the voice instantly, and he didn't wait for me to take the few steps into the living room, instead stomping into the kitchen and bumping into me as I rushed to meet him.

"Pawpaw! I just made some chicken if you—"

"Don't you dare say another fucking word to me. I've heard a lot of shit going 'round town that I *never* thought I'd hear about you." Behind him, the sky saturated to a murky ocean green, and against it his face glowed as red as a poker fresh from the fire. My lips trembled but I couldn't get any words to come out. He leaned closer, his breath sour with the stink of cheap beer and dip. "Now don't try to deny any of it. I know you ran off Travis yourself. I've heard from several neighbors that they saw his semi pull up the other day and then leave again in a hurry. Why'd you lie?" He grabbed my shoulders, shaking me. "What'd you do?"

"Leave her alone," June spoke up behind me.

"Shut up, you whore. Get outta this house."

June didn't say another word, her face blank, moving slow and calm past us and out the front door.

I swallowed hard and he turned his attention back to me. "I'm cuttin' you off, and I expect you to sell this place and get me my down payment back right away. You can't stay here."

"But Pawpaw—"

"Shut your fucking mouth!" His calloused palm flew hard against my cheek, the rough patches cutting through my soft skin as my head was thrown to the right. "You're outta the will too. Not getting a goddamn cent from me, you stinkin' Delilah."

"I don't want your money anyway! I got plenty." Another slap sent me reeling the second the words left my mouth.

"From what? Stealing? Whoring? Is this what you're gonna be now? A goddamn whore like that farmhand you're always hanging around with? Everybody knows what kind of girl she is, and now she's ruined you. That's why Travis ran off. You've disgraced me, Libby. Shamed our whole family." His voice devolved into an animal growl. "It's unnatural."

That's when the real blows began, but I hadn't anticipated it, so I didn't brace myself at all, instead struck to the ground like a newborn whelp. The punches rained down along with the rhythm of the storm, and I thought to pray for mercy, maybe a miracle, but decided against it. There was no point. June was right. Abandoned, I curled into myself and waited for him to tire.

Outside, the wind whistled and howled something fierce, tearing at the few trees and skittering away with anything light and not anchored down. Past the stinging pain in my eyes, the wash of unsettling green through the window hit me.

"Pawpaw," I croaked, "We've gotta get in the bathroom. Tornado's coming."

"I'm not hiding in any bathroom with trash like you. I'd rather take my chances with the tornado." A shadow passed over his features. "I hope it hits here and takes you with it. You can burn in Hell where you belong."

"Take it back," I whimpered, lip trembling and fingers reaching toward him.

He looked at me and spat on the floor. There wasn't a glimmer of love left in his eyes.

"Well, I might burn, but you're the goddamn Devil himself!" The words sputtered out, shocking me as they roared alongside the storm.

But my shouting didn't slow his exit. It was as if he hadn't even heard me. Just as he reached the doorway, June's wild mane appeared at the sliding glass door. She threw it open and stormed inside.

I tried to scream out something to stop her, but my voice rang out hollow and hoarse. It was too late. Pawpaw was yelling more curses at her when she plunged the knife deep into his shoulder. He shrieked and writhed from her, not letting her retrieve it, so she grabbed a chair from the table, lifted it over his head, and brought it down with enough force that he toppled to his knees. His hands raised over his head, attempting to form a protective shell, but June brought the broken mess of splinters down on him again and again, his grunts mingling with the cracking of both bones and wood. Each strike brought him lower until the old man was curled in on himself like a pill bug, his façade exposed, frail, pathetic, and whimpering softly. June still didn't let up. As the chair broke apart completely, leaving only a wooden leg in her hand, she looked at it a moment then thrust it down into the soft of his belly, staking him and bringing it up only to thrust it into him again, the end now dripping bright red. Pawpaw didn't move.

When June finished, she tossed the chair leg against the wall where it smacked and left a stamp of blood. She turned to me panting with a string of spit dribbling off her bottom lip which she swiped away with her sleeve.

"Don't look at me like that. You're free now. Understand?"

"But what are we gonna do now?"

She took my face in her hands.

"Anything we want."

As she spoke, the cruel face who'd slain three

men in front of me, one whom I loved like a father, disappeared, leaving only beautiful June. The girl I'd spent night after night with, sharing dreams and whispering secrets into her perfumed hair. We crashed into each other, one beast of hands and lips and tender skin. My grandfather's blood was splattered across her body, smearing onto me, anointing me in our shared sin, but in this moment, I didn't care. She'd done it all for me.

The roaring grew louder, and under June's hand, I inched closer to revelation. She whispered nothings in my ear, but I could scarcely hear over the beating wind and rain. I turned my head and out the window, far across the cotton fields, was the swirling gray whip of a thin tornado against the jade sky. I held my breath and I saw my own rain-streaked reflection, a ghost image between the twister and me. Streams of water ran down the glass across my blood-stained face and I was struck by sick, sublime clarity. It hummed through my flesh with a powerful sadness like I'd never felt before. I had no more doubts. I was staring at the face of God.

acknowledgments

Thank you so much to everyone who made this book possible. I'm especially thankful for my early readers Steve Neal, Evelyn Freeling, Katrina Carruth, Lor Gislason, Shelley Lavigne, and especially Mae Murray, who encouraged me to expand this story to its full potential. A huge thank you to my wonderful husband Martin for encouraging me to follow my writing dreams, always supporting me, taking the early baby shift so I can stay up late to write, and for reading all of it and giving thoughtful feedback (even though you can't stand horror). Thank you Alan Lastufka for believing in this little story and giving it a chance as well as a beautiful cover. Thank you to my sisters, Tara and Hannah, for being my biggest cheerleaders and always there to bounce ideas off of, and finally, thank you to my dad for fostering my love of reading and teaching me that horrific southern phrase for a sun shower that inspired this whole story.

about the author

Emma E. Murray's work has appeared in anthologies like *What One Wouldn't Do, Obsolescence*, and *Ooze: Little Bursts of Body Horror* as well as magazines such as *Cosmic Horror Monthly, If There's Anyone Left, Pyre,* and *Vastarien*. Her chapbook, *Exquisite Hunger,* is available from Medusa Haus, her debut novel *Crushing Snails* (Apocalypse Party) will be out August 2024, and her novel *Shoot Me in the Face on a Beautiful Day* (Apocalypse Party) will be coming out summer 2025. To read more, you can visit her website EmmaEMurray.com

a note from shortwave publishing

Thank you for reading!

If you enjoyed this Shortwave title, please consider writing a review. Reviews help readers find more titles they may enjoy, and that helps us continue to publish more titles like this.

OUR WEBSITE
shortwavepublishing.com

SOCIAL MEDIA
@ShortwaveBooks

EMAIL US
contact@shortwavepublishing.com

content warnings

- violence
- murder (poisoning and beating)
- domestic violence
- death

9 781959 565307